Someday

alison mcghee    peter h. reynolds

# Someday

ATHENEUM BOOKS FOR YOUNG READERS    New York   London   Toronto   Sydney

One day I counted your fingers
and kissed each one.

One day the first snowflakes fell, and I held you up

and watched them melt on your baby skin.

One day
we crossed the street,
and you held my hand tight.

Then, you were my baby.

and now you are my child.

Sometimes, when you sleep, I watch you dream,

and I dream too....

That someday you will dive into the

Cool, clear water of a lake.

Someday
you will walk
into a deep wood.

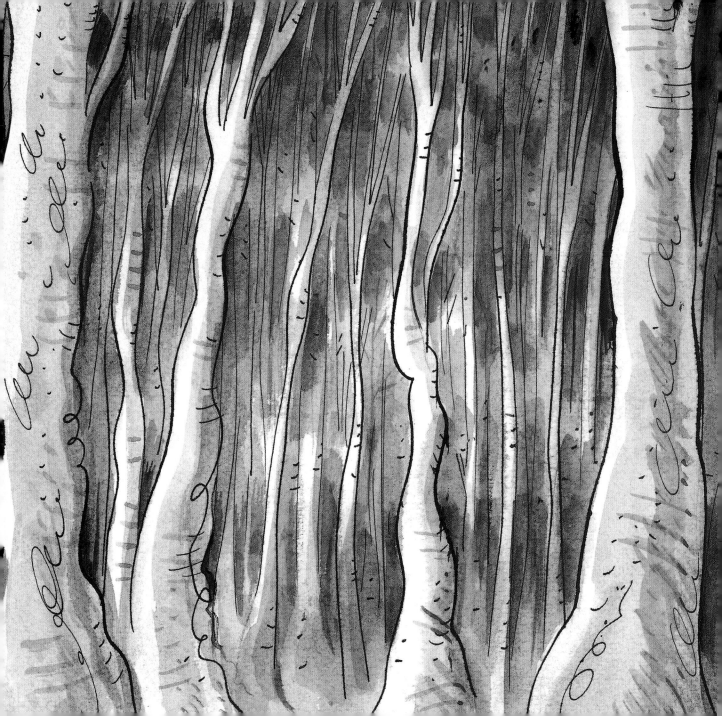

Someday your eyes

will be filled with a joy so deep that they shine.

Someday you

Will run so fast and so far your heart will feel like fire.

Someday you will swing high – so high,

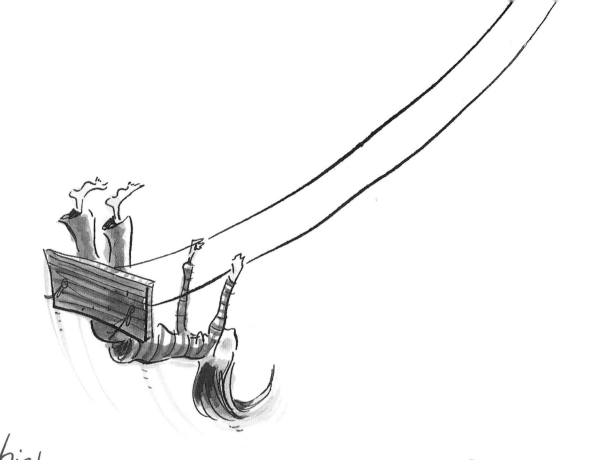

higher than you ever dared to swing.

Someday
You will hear something so sad
that you will fold up
with sorrow.

Someday you will call a song to the wind,

and the wind will carry your song away.

Someday I will stand on this porch

and watch your arms waving to me until I no longer see you.

Someday you will look at this house and

Wonder how something that feels so big can look so small.

Someday you will feel
a small weight
against your strong back.

Someday I will watch you brushing your child's hair.

Someday, a long time from now, your own hair will glow silver in the sun.

And when that day comes, love,

you will remember me.

*To Gabrielle Kirsch McGhee,*
*with love and respect*
*—A. M.*

*To the Queen Mother of our Family,*
*the very wise and beautiful*
*Hazel Gasson Reynolds*
*—P. H. R.*

Atheneum Books for Young Readers
An imprint of Simon & Schuster
Children's Publishing Division
1230 Avenue of the Americas
New York, New York 10020
Text copyright © 2007 by
Alison McGhee
Illustrations copyright © 2007 by
Peter H. Reynolds
All rights reserved, including the right
of reproduction in whole or in part in
any form.
Book design by Ann Bobco
The text for this book is handlettered
by Peter H. Reynolds.
The illustrations for this book
are rendered in pen and ink and
watercolor.
Printed in China

30 29 28 27 26 25 24 23 22 21
Library of Congress Cataloging-in-
Publication Data
Someday / Alison McGhee ;
illustrated by Peter H. Reynolds. —1st
ed.
p.  cm.
Summary: A mother reflects on all the
milestones, from walking in a deep
wood to brushing someone else's hair,
that her child will achieve during life.
ISBN-13: 978-1-4169-2811-9
ISBN-10: 1-4169-2811-1
[1. Mother and child—Fiction.]
I. Reynolds, Peter, 1961–, ill.
II. Title.
PZ7.M4784675Soe 2007
[E]—dc22
2006003904

0216 SCP